One Big Adventure

Cally Gee

CWR

Editing, design and production by CWR.
Cover image: Cally Gee and CWR
Printed in the UK by Linney.
ISBN: 978-1-78259-838-1

PRINTED MAY 2018

This book is dedicated to
Lola, Max, Finn, Asha, Nate,
Woody, Rocco, Asha, Tilly and
Seb – I think you are all so brave.

Thank you for modelling courage,
adventure and bravery to me. You
are very special children and I'm
excited to see your life adventures
take shape.

I would like to acknowledge
all those who helped me to understand
book-world terminology! Mark, Scot,
Bryony and Angela – you are super
skilled and I am sincerely grateful for your
wisdom, help and support.

I would especially like to thank
my Dream Team, FC and D-Group,
as well as Harriet, Sabs, Maverick,
Caroline, and Verity. Your own
courage, support, friendship and
help has been so valuable to me.
Thank you.

Dear Mini Friend,

Hello! Welcome to another **Miniphant & Me** book.

My friends and I love learning new things and going on adventures, and you can come too!

Our stories talk about:

thoughts in our head...

feelings in our heart...

and actions with our body...

because the way we think changes the way we feel and what we choose to do.

See if you can spot these in the story!

I hope you enjoy adventuring with me as I learn to think about the things I do differently. You will see that thinking this way helps me to be stronger than I feel, because of the courage I find to become braver! You can do it too.

In the Animal Friend Fact Files at the back of this book, my friends and I share some of the ways in which we practise becoming braver. You will also find some Bedtime Thoughts for when you are getting ready to go to sleep and some activities you can do called Daytime Fun, for when it's a good time to play. I'll come and find you at the end of the story to tell you more about them.

Have fun!

Love, **Miniphant** x

One last thing... every time I have shown bravery, courage or strength in the story, there is a special badge called a 'medal' hiding in the picture. Can you find them all?

'I'm packing for an adventure!' came a muffled voice from inside the sleeping bag. 'I need to fit all this in my suitcase,' Miniphant said, poking his head out.

Robin's head shook doubtfully. Miniphant tried anyway.

Miniphant folded, flattened, poked and prodded.

He pushed, pulled, squashed and squeezed.

The day went, and evening came. Finally, wobbling on all fours on top of his suitcase, Miniphant trumped out of both ends. **'I've done it!'** he said.

'Oopsie-poopsie-pardon, I've done it,' he said again, still wobbling. 'My suitcase is packed. I'm ready for an adventure!'

Meanwhile, Cat had been watching from the comfort of the house. Even though going outside meant getting her lovely clean paws muddy, she jumped through the cat-flap and into the garden.

'Off you go then,' she meowed meanly.

'I... I can't,' said Miniphant, realising that if he got off the suitcase, it was sure to burst open.

'What's wrong, Miniphant?' Cat continued (knowing full well what was wrong).

'My suitcase won't stay shut!' Miniphant cried. He was tired of packing, and just wanted to go on his adventure.

'Well, you're not going to get far like that, are you?' Cat purred cruelly. Although she was being very unkind, Cat was right.

Miniphant's trunk and ears drooped as the truth of Cat's words sunk in. Feeling cold, tired and very hungry, he climbed sadly off his suitcase and walked into the shed. Behind him came the sounds of...

whoosh

BANG

thump and

...before they came crashing back down all over the grass.

as the suitcase exploded, sending Miniphant's hopes of adventure flying high up into the air...

Miniphant curled up in his ice cream tub house, with tears in his eyes and hurt in his heart. **'I'll try again tomorrow,'** he sniffed. **'Perhaps I'm not meant to go on an adventure?'** he wondered, his hopeful thinking turning to doubt.

A big wet tear of disappointment rolled down his trunk. Miniphant whispered his prayers and muddled thoughts into his pillow and went to sleep.

The next day, he woke up to the sound of Robin and Mole outside.
'Ah, there you are, Miniphant!' said Robin.
'We were just saying how brave you are!'
'Brave?' said Miniphant, feeling confused and surprised. 'How is <u>not</u> doing something being brave?'

'You gave it a go, Miniphant,' Mole smiled.
'But it didn't work! You heard what Cat said, and she was right,' replied Miniphant.
'It didn't work – <u>yet</u>,' Mole encouraged.
'Maybe you just need to think about it all in a different way,' suggested Robin.

Miniphant thought that doing a headstand would be a different way of thinking about it.

'So, yesterday's packing... and then Cat's unkindness... actually <u>helped</u> me to become brave?' he thought aloud, balancing upside down.

'It was difficult to pack everything into my suitcase, but I tried really hard,' Miniphant continued.

'I was worried about making everything that I <u>thought</u> I needed fit, but strong thinking helped me to believe I could do it, so I kept trying. I was thinking so much about what I needed to take, that I forgot who I needed to become!' he trumped, the thoughts becoming clearer in his head.

'I guess it <u>was</u> brave to try something new. And it was strong to walk away from Cat. But it didn't <u>feel</u> like that. All of it took courage... COURAGE! Courage is having strong thinking to believe you can do something, even if you feel fearful! And that helps you to be brave!'

Suddenly, Miniphant knew what he really needed.

Toppling over in excitement, he shouted triumphantly,

'Courage is what I need to take on an adventure! It's not so much about the stuff you pack – it's what you carry in your heart and think in your head that will help you in life's adventures! Isn't that right, Robin?'

Robin nodded, astonished and impressed by Miniphant's upside-down thinking.

Miniphant jumped up, flung open the suitcase lid, and wrote in big letters across it: **COURAGE.**

'**I put on <u>courage</u> and I carry it with me into my adventures,**' he said happily, already feeling stronger and acting braver.

'I must thank Cat!' Miniphant said. It was Robin's turn to be confused and surprised. '<u>Thank</u> Cat? She should be saying <u>sorry</u> to YOU!' Robin twittered.

'Cat was mean and hurtful,' explained Miniphant, 'but what she said was true. I wasn't going anywhere on top of the suitcase...

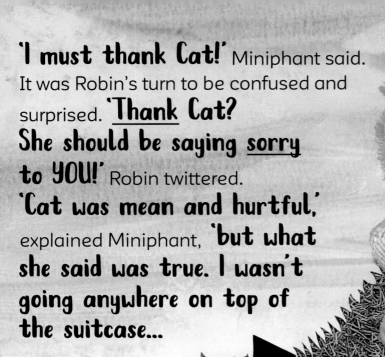

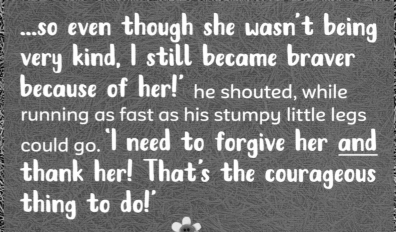

...so even though she wasn't being very kind, I still became braver because of her!' he shouted, while running as fast as his stumpy little legs could go. 'I need to forgive her <u>and</u> thank her! That's the courageous thing to do!'

Miniphant felt fear wobble in his tummy as he reached the cat-flap. He could hear his heart beating in his head. Panting to catch his breath and picking up his suitcase full of courage, he bravely climbed through. Before Miniphant even realised it, he was having an adventure after all!

Mole and Robin watched from outside the window, amazed at how brave and courageous their little friend had become.

Cat was too proud to say sorry. But Miniphant's courage grew stronger as he forgave and thanked her anyway.

'Well done, Miniphant!' his friends cheered, as they headed back down the garden path together.

Miniphant felt tired, but braver. 'I think that's enough adventuring for one day,' he said. 'I'm hungry!'

'You're ALWAYS hungry!' giggled Mole.

'You need food to give you energy to keep on being brave and courageous. Life is ONE BIG ADVENTURE, Miniphant!' Robin sang.

'Oh, goodie!' said Miniphant, rubbing his tummy. 'That means MORE food!' He trumped happily out of both ends...

'Oopsie-poopsie-pardon!'

They all laughed.

Brave and Courageous Animal Friend Fact Files

It took courage for me to think about things in a different way after my first tries at packing had gone wrong. It took even more courage to admit that Cat had been right and to forgive her unkind words.

Wow, Miniphant, your incredible courage has made you braver!

I really like being clean and dry, so my friends know that it takes courage for me to go out into the garden where my paws and fur can get dirty and wet. My courage and strong thinking help me to practise doing this, using my 'cat-flap' (a special door allowing me to go in and out at any time – day or night!).

Wow, Cat, you have become wonderfully brave!

My friends think I am brave because I can fly *and* read! It took courage and hard work for me to learn these skills, but I asked for help and practised every day until I got the hang of it. Believing positive things helped me to grow the courage and strong thinking I needed to keep on trying.

Wow, Robin, you have become brilliantly brave!

I live on my own, underground and in the dark, and it takes courage for me to come outside. But because I chose to be courageous, I'm now friends with Cat, Robin and Miniphant! We love spending time together, and would really miss each other if I didn't come out to play!

Wow, Mole, your fantastic courage has made you brave!

Bedtime Thoughts and Daytime Fun

Hello again Mini Friend,
   I hope you enjoyed the story!
   Did you find all the medals showing the times I was brave, strong and courageous?
   What was it that I worked out we really need to take with us on adventures?
Here are some more fun things we can do together...

Bedtime Thoughts

Grown-ups: you can use these thinking, whispering, and listening activities as part of the bedtime routine, enhancing your child's emotional literacy, mental health and spiritual wellbeing. They are designed to be calming and settling, thought provoking and comforting at the end of the day.

Emotional Literacy

To talk about

Bravery is doing something without showing fear.
Courage is doing something even when you feel fearful about it.
   Sometimes we have worried feelings because we don't know how things will turn out, so our thoughts become fearful too. Fearful thoughts are what gave Miniphant the wobbly feeling in his tummy. But he quickly chose to think strong and be courageous by going through the cat-flap anyway.
   Believing in your head that you can do something, even if you don't feel it in your body yet, is thinking positively and bravely. Miniphant calls this 'strong thinking'. It gives you 'inside strength' to help you be courageous to *do* something, even if you *feel* afraid.

To do

Whisper together how fear feels to you. Give each other a hug. It's OK to *feel* afraid, but it's great to encourage each other to not *be* afraid.
   Look for ways in which you can practise being courageous every day, to help you think strong and become braver.

Mental Health

To talk about

Thinking brave thoughts gives us courage and 'inside strength' to do something difficult. Talk about something you feel afraid of doing. Together, think of an action you could do, or a thought to remember, or some special words you could say that will help you to think bravely and start climbing on top of those fears. (Miniphant likes to stomp on his fears once he's climbed on top of them. You can too, if you like.)

To do

Think about all the positive (happy, good) 'thought and feeling' words you could pack in your own imaginary suitcase, along with courage.

Can you say one thought about yourself that is true, that you think is lovely and good? One thing you think is the best and not the worst? One thing that you think is beautiful and not horrible? One thing – or many things! – you are thankful for?

Practising positive thinking about yourself and the world around you will help you grow stronger on the inside and become ready for courageous and fun life adventures on the outside. Try it as you fall asleep.

Spiritual Wellbeing

To talk about

Do you remember how, after Miniphant's difficult day, he went to bed feeling sad, disappointed and hurt? The story says, 'He whispered his prayers and muddled thoughts into his pillow'. Knowing how Miniphant felt, what do you think he whispered?

If you look in another book called the Bible, you will read that Miniphant's friend, Jesus, says that you can talk to Him when you are feeling tired and have lots of thoughts in your head and feelings in your heart. He will help you and give you the rest you need. It also says that He knows when you sit down and when you stand up. He knows all your thoughts and exactly how you feel. In fact, He knows everything that happens in your life – day and night.

To do

It feels good to know that Jesus knows and understands *all* our thoughts, feelings and actions. Why not try saying your own prayer? Jesus loves it when we talk to Him. That's what prayer is – talking to Jesus. It also says in the Bible that God has made us to be strong and courageous, so we don't have to be afraid of anything because He is with us. When Jesus talks about being 'strong', He doesn't mean you need big muscles on your arms. He's talking about an 'inside strength' that comes from thinking in your head, and believing in your heart that with His help, you can do *anything*. He knows that you may *feel* afraid sometimes, but He says you don't need to *be* afraid, because He is always with you and He is bigger than all our fears. The more we remember this, the stronger and more courageous we'll be and the braver we'll become.

Daytime Fun

Grown-ups: designed to be interactive, fun and creative, these activities can be integrated into your child's day to enhance their physical awareness, social understanding and creative thinking.

Physical Activity: Face the Feeling

To do

One player starts their turn as the 'Face-maker': they make a face in the mirror, look at it and then make the same face to the 'Guesser', who must guess the feeling the face is making. Then swap over. Continue taking it in turns to express as many different feelings as possible. The next level is to see if the children can use their whole body to show a feeling.

To talk about

Ask them if they know someone who looks like this sometimes. What might make that person feel this way? This activity is all about physical recognition of feelings in themselves and others, helping the children to see how we express those feelings with our faces and by our actions.

Social Activity: Act a Different Way

To talk about

Cat may have told the truth, but the *way* she said it was full of pride, and not very kind. She was thinking about making herself look better than the others, wanting the attention to be on her for knowing the answer – rather than helping Miniphant to find *his* answer to the packing problem. Cat made Miniphant look silly and laughed at him, rather than helping and encouraging him (which is what a good friend would have done). She was jealous and selfish in her thinking, which made her mean and unkind in her words and actions.

Have you ever been unkind because you were feeling jealous (wanting all the attention), or thought you were better than someone else (being too proud) or were only thinking about yourself (being selfish)? Has anyone else ever been unkind to you in those ways? It doesn't feel very good, does it? Let's try to encourage each other with kind words and actions, and let's always be willing to say sorry when we forget to be kind.

To do

Pretend that one of you is Cat and one of you is Miniphant. Act out this part of the story, making up a kinder way in which Cat could have still told Miniphant the truth without being hurtful and selfish. Take turns, so that everyone gets the chance to act out being both Cat and Miniphant.

Creative Activity: Make a Medal

To talk about

Sometimes, when people do very brave things they are given a medal to say, 'Wow, you were so brave!' A medal is like a special badge that you wear.

To do

Make your own medal, like the ones you found in the story, using cardboard or paper. You can find a handy template for these on the website. You could decorate it with ribbon, draw a picture in the middle or ask for help to write the word *brave* or *courageous* on it. To make it look extra special, you could use foil or shiny paper.

   Grown-ups: Use these home-made medals as part of a self-esteem and confidence building chart (or visual timetable) when reflecting on the day. Ask the child or children: 'When did you feel you were being brave or courageous today?' Tell them about any moments when you noticed them being brave or courageous. Explain that in those moments, they were actually wearing an invisible medal. They might not have realised it at the time, but now looking back over the day, they can see it. The medal can be moved beside the timetable, where and when these brave or courageous moments took place. Or you can simply stick the medal on a piece of blank paper, and write or draw the 'medal moments' next to it. Helping your child to visually link bravery and courage to the everyday decisions they make will help boost their self-worth, and soon they will begin to recognise these moments for themselves!

It's time to say goodbye for now, Mini Friend. It's been great learning about courage and becoming brave with you! Remember to wear your invisibility medals and be a great friend. That way you'll help other people to think strong, and be brave and courageous too!

See you **oopsie-poopsie** soon!
Love,

Join Miniphant and friends for more adventures in

Miniphant Moves In
and
The Magnificent Raspberry Mountain

For more information about the **Miniphant & Me** series,
including additional Bedtime Thoughts, Daytime Fun and lots more, visit

www.cwr.org.uk/miniphant